AMERICAN TALL TALES

Pecos Bill

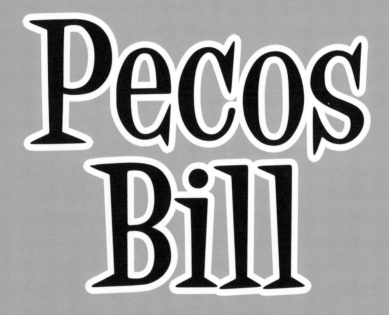

Retold by M. J. York ❧ Illustrated by Michael Garland

The Child's World®
1980 Lookout Drive • Mankato, MN 56003-1705
800-599-READ • www.childsworld.com

Acknowledgments
The Child's World®: Mary Berendes, Publishing Director
The Design Lab: Kathleen Petelinsek, Design
Red Line Editorial: Editorial direction

ISBN 9781614732129
LCCN 2012932869

Printed in the United States of America
Mankato, MN
January 2013
PA02166

Way back in the days when the West was wild, the bravest, toughest baby north of the Rio Grande was born to pioneer parents. Now, this baby's name was William, but everyone called him Baby Bill.

Even in the cradle, everyone knew Baby Bill would grow up to be somethin' special. Why,

when he was barely toddlin',
Baby Bill would have played
rattles with rattlesnakes and toy
soldiers with scorpions if his ma
woulda let him. When he started
to crawl, he'd sneak out of the
cabin and wander off to wrestle
baby bear cubs.

One day, Baby Bill started
cryin' and fussin' something
terrible. His mam tried everything,
but nothing she did calmed him
down. Finally, Bill's oldest brother,
Bobby, figured it out. Another

family had moved in fifty miles away, and Baby Bill was feeling crowded. Ma and Pop agreed with Baby Bill, so they packed up the family in a covered wagon and headed west toward the sunset.

Not long into their journey, the family had to ford the wide, wild Pecos River. The wagon jammed against a rock, and Baby Bill popped out the back afore anyone noticed. Luckily, Baby Bill taught himself how to swim right quick. But the family traveled on and

didn't notice he was missin' until it was too late. It's from that tricky river that Baby Bill got his new nickname, Pecos Bill.

So, Pecos Bill crawled out of the river and took off crawling through the Texas sand. He might have crawled clear back to the old cabin, but he crawled smack dab into a coyote. Now, this coyote was a momma coyote. She looked at the dirty, naked pink thing crawling at her and wondered if her cubs would like it for supper.

But then Pecos Bill sat up and started scratching her behind the ear. "Nice doggy," he said.

The momma coyote's heart melted a little. The pink thing was kinda cute after all. She took him home to her den, but instead of eating him for supper she decided to raise him with her coyote cubs.

So Pecos Bill spent the next seventeen years runnin' with the coyotes. When they howled at the moon, he howled around with them. When they hunted, he chased prey clear across the prairie with them. He learned how to read scents on the wind and how to stay so still he turned invisible.

It was a fine, hot day in the middle of the summer and Pecos Bill was playin' tag with some prairie dogs when he saw an unfamiliar sight. A tall creature

was comin' toward him through the tall grass. Pecos Bill couldn't tell if it had four legs or six. It had been so long since he'd seen a man on a horse, he'd forgotten what one looked like.

The cowboy hauled back on the reins and stopped short when he saw Pecos Bill. He was dirty and sunburned and naked as the day he was born. But the cowboy squinted at Pecos Bill then started cryin' and carryin' on with joy. You see, the cowboy was Bob, Bill's oldest brother, and he recognized Pecos Bill. Bill had grown to look mighty like their mother. She had died of grief seventeen years earlier from losin' her baby boy.

However, Pecos Bill needed more convincing that he'd met his long-lost brother. Problem was, Pecos Bill thought he was a coyote. He just looked at his brother and howled.

"If you're a coyote, where's your tail?" argued Bob.

Pecos Bill looked over his shoulder and started turning in circles trying to see his tail. At last he said, "Well, I'm beat. Guess I'm a man after all."

So Bill followed Bob back to the ranch, where Bob said he'd make him the best cowboy Texas had ever seen. At first, though, Pecos Bill thought it was hard being a man. For one thing, clothes are mighty scratchy if you aren't used to wearin' them. And using a knife, a fork, and a

spoon instead of your hands takes some gettin' used to.

But one thing Pecos Bill did take to right away was horses. It could be they smelled the coyote in him and respected him for it. Or maybe they knew he was wilder than them. Whatever it was, there wasn't a horse in the West that Pecos Bill couldn't tame.

Pecos Bill was on his way to town to buy himself a new horse when he passed a herd of wild mustangs. The other cowboys yelled that the mustangs were too wild and they'd kick his head in. But Pecos Bill ran up to the wildest horse in the herd and hopped aboard bareback. And hoo-wee did that horse kick and buck up a storm. He bucked so hard he turned somersaults. But Bill stuck on his back like a burr.

Finally exhausted, the horse gave up. He looked over his shoulder at Pecos Bill and gave him a friendly little nip on the knee. Bill knew from that

moment they'd be the best of
friends. He called his new friend
Widow-Maker 'cuz no other
cowboy could ride him.

Pecos Bill was the best cowboy
in Texas, and he taught the other
cowboys some better ways of
doing things. He taught them
to tie a loop at the end of a rope
and use it to lasso down cows.
He taught them to ride herd
and keep the cows together in a
group. And he even taught them
to sing cowboy songs around the

campfire at night, singing at the moon like he'd done as a coyote.

One summer, Texas was in the middle of the worst drought anyone could remember. The Pecos River ran almost dry, and even the cacti shriveled up and blew away. There was no water for the cows and horses.

But Pecos Bill knew just what to do. Up in Oklahoma, a huge tornado, black and mighty, was twisting away on the prairie and keeping the rain clouds with it.

Pecos Bill galloped Widow-Maker up to Oklahoma and found that twister. Pecos Bill took his rope—the longest in Texas—tossed it through the air, and lassoed the twister right out of the sky. He jumped on top and rode that twister all the way back to Texas, jabbing it with his spurs to make it rain as he went.

So the drought ended in Texas, and Pecos Bill invented the rodeo. Though today, most cowboys ride horses and bulls in the rodeo, not tornadoes.

BEYOND THE STORY

Pecos Bill is a classic example of the American tall tale. Tall tales can be based on truth or completely fictional, but they always include unbelievable, or exaggerated, elements in real places like the American West.

If you didn't already guess, the Pecos Bill character is fictional, or entirely made up. But it sure is fun to read his story and imagine such things happening: being raised by a coyote family, learning to leap like an antelope, lassoing a cyclone.

People say author Edward O'Reilly first wrote about Pecos Bill in the early 1900s, based on the tales of cowboys and ranch workers he'd hear around campfires.

Though the things that Pecos Bill accomplishes in this story may be impossible to do in real life, we can learn from his courage and strength. American pioneers who had to live off the land as they moved West for the first time had to be courageous and strong like Pecos Bill. He shows us many other traits, however exaggerated, that are also true of the American pioneer spirit. He is resourceful: traveling to Oklahoma to bring rain back to Texas. He is sharing: teaching others new ways to do things, like lassoing, herding cows, and singing campfire songs.

There are many other stories of Pecos Bill. Some tell of him riding a mountain lion instead of a horse; others tell of him eating dynamite, supposedly his favorite food! Can you imagine being that tough?

ABOUT THE AUTHOR

M. J. York has an undergraduate degree in English and history and a master's degree in library science. M. J. lives in Minnesota and works as a children's book editor. She has always been fascinated by myths, legends, and fairy tales from around the world.

ABOUT THE ILLUSTRATOR

Michael Garland is a best-selling author and illustrator with thirty books to his credit. He has received numerous awards and his recent book, *Miss Smith and the Haunted Library*, made the New York Times Best Sellers list. Michael has illustrated for celebrity authors such as James Patterson and Gloria Estefan, and his book *Christmas Magic* has become a season classic. Michael lives in New York with his family.